MR. QUIET

by Roger Hargreaves

D1454135

Mr Quiet liked the quiet life.

He lived, quietly, in a small little cottage in the middle of a wood.

The problem was, that small little cottage was in the middle of a wood in the middle of a country called Loudland!

Everything and everybody in Loudland was noisy.

Oh, the noise!

Dogs didn't go "woof" like dogs you know.

They went (take a deep breath) "WOOF!"

People didn't shut their doors like you or I would shut our doors.

They slammed them.

BANG!

People didn't talk to each other.

They shouted at each other.

"HELLO," they'd shout as they met in the street.

And, you've heard about something being as quiet as a mouse, haven't you?

Not in Loudland.

They had the noisiest mice in the world.

"SQUEAK! SQUEAK!" they'd roar at each other.

Mr Noisy would have liked living in Loudland.

He'd have loved it.

But Mr Quiet didn't.

Noise frightened him.

So, he stayed in his cottage in the middle of his wood as much as he could.

But of course he couldn't stay there all the time.

Every week, for instance, he had to go shopping.

He used to creep into the grocer's shop.

"GOOD MORNING," bellowed the grocer.
"WHAT CAN I DO FOR YOU?"

"Please," whispered Mr Quiet, "could I have some cornflakes please?"

"WHAT?"

"Cornflakes. Please," he whispered.

"SPEAK UP!"

Mr Quiet tried his loudest whisper.

"Cornflakes."

"CAN'T HEAR YOU," shouted the grocer. "NEXT PLEASE!"

And poor Mr Quiet had to creep away without any cornflakes.

It wasn't fair, was it?

He crept into the butcher's.

"Please," he whispered, "I'd like some meat."

The butcher didn't even hear him.

He was humming to himself, loudly and fiercely.

Mr Quiet tried again.

"Please," he whispered, "I'd like some meat."

The butcher started to whistle.

It sounded more like a burglar alarm than a whistle.

Mr Quiet fled.

Empty handed.

It often happened, which probably explains why he was so little.

Poor Mr Quiet.

He sat at home that night with a feeling of despair.

"Whatever am I to do?" he thought.

"It's no use," he thought, "I'll just have to try again."

And so, the following day, he went shopping again.

But, the same thing happened.

"CAN'T HEAR YOU," thundered the grocer. "NEXT PLEASE!"

"CAN'T HEAR YOU," bellowed the greengrocer. "NEXT PLEASE!"

"CAN'T HEAR YOU," roared the milkman. "NEXT PLEASE!"

"CAN'T HEAR YOU," boomed the butcher. "NEXT PLEASE!"

Oh dear!

Poor Mr Quiet went home and went to bed.

Hungry.

The morning after he was awakened by a noise which sounded like bombs dropping.

It was the Loudland postman knocking at Mr Quiet's door.

BANG! BANG! BANG! BANG!

Mr Quiet went and opened the door.

"MORNING," shouted the postman. "LETTER FOR YOU!"

Mr Quiet took the letter into his kitchen.

He sat down to open it.

He waited until the noise of the postman's footsteps died away.

CLUMP CLUMP CLUMP CLUMP clump clump.

Mr Quiet opened the letter in great excitement.

He'd never had a letter before.

It was from Mr Happy in Happyland.

An invitation!

To stay!

Mr Quiet was overjoyed.

He rushed upstairs and packed his bag and set off that very morning.

It was late when he arrived on Mr Happy's doorstep.

He knocked on Mr Happy's door.

Tap tap tap.

Mr Happy opened the door.

"Hello," he smiled. "I thought I heard something. You must be Mr Quiet. Well, don't just stand there, come in and have some supper."

It was the first proper meal Mr Quiet had had for months. And while he was eating it he told Mr Happy all about the problems he'd been having in Loudland.

Mr Happy was most sympathetic.

Over breakfast the following morning, Mr Happy told Mr Quiet that he'd been thinking about his problem.

"I think," he said, "that under the circumstances you'd better stay here in Happyland."

Mr Quiet's face lit up.

"And," continued Mr Happy, "we'll find you a house, and," he went on, "a job."

Mr Quiet's face dropped.

"I'm not very good at jobs," he confessed, "because I'm too quiet."

"Ah," smiled Mr Happy. "I have the very job for a quiet chap like you!"

And so, the very next day, Mr Quiet started work.

And he loves it.

Do you know where he works?

In the Happy Lending Library!

As you know, everybody who goes into a library has to be very quiet, and only whispering is allowed.

What a clever idea of Mr Happy's, wasn't it?

And these days, Mr Quiet is as happy as can be.

Why, only the other day, do you know what he did on his way home from work?

He was so happy he laughed out loud.

Can you imagine?

Tee hee hee!

"NEXT PLEASE!"